sleepover fun with llama llama!

a sticker & activity book

Anna Dewdney

Based on the bestselling children's book series
by Anna Dewdney

PENGUIN YOUNG READERS LICENSES
An Imprint of Penguin Random House LLC

Published by Penguin Young Readers Licenses, an imprint of
Penguin Random House LLC, 345 Hudson Street,
New York, New York 10014. Manufactured in China.

ISBN 9781524785048   10 9 8 7 6 5 4 3 2 1

Llama Llama is excited to go to his first-ever sleepover!

He is going to Gilroy's house.

Can you help him and Mama find the way?

Start

Finish

At Gilroy's house, Llama goes swimming and helps with chores.
Can you finish the scene by coloring in Llama and his friends?

After all the swimming and chores, Llama sure is hungry! Time for dinner with Gilroy's family.

Finish the scene with stickers.

Don't forget to add lots of new foods for Llama to try!

The food is not the same as the food at home. Llama decides to make himself a special plate. Llama's plate is a lot like Euclid's, but some things are different. Can you find the five differences?

After dinner, Llama, Gilroy, and Euclid catch fireflies.
How many did they catch? Count the fireflies in all three jars.

Answer:

Time to get ready for bed! The whole group changes into their pajamas and starts brushing their teeth.

Color in their pajamas.

Be sure to make Llama's pajamas red!

Even though Euclid and Gilroy don't know Llama Llama's brushing song, they all know how to make toothpaste mustaches!

Use the stickers provided to finish the scene by adding their toothpaste mustaches.

Before they go to sleep, Gilroy helps his friends do a monster check. Luckily, there are no monsters! "Looks like we're monster-free," Gilroy says.

Gilroy then shows Llama his night-light and his stuffed animals.

Add stickers to complete Gilroy's room!

All the boys are sleeping when suddenly: **ROAR!** Gilroy's brother runs into the room in a scary monster costume!

Connect the dots to complete the scary monster costume.

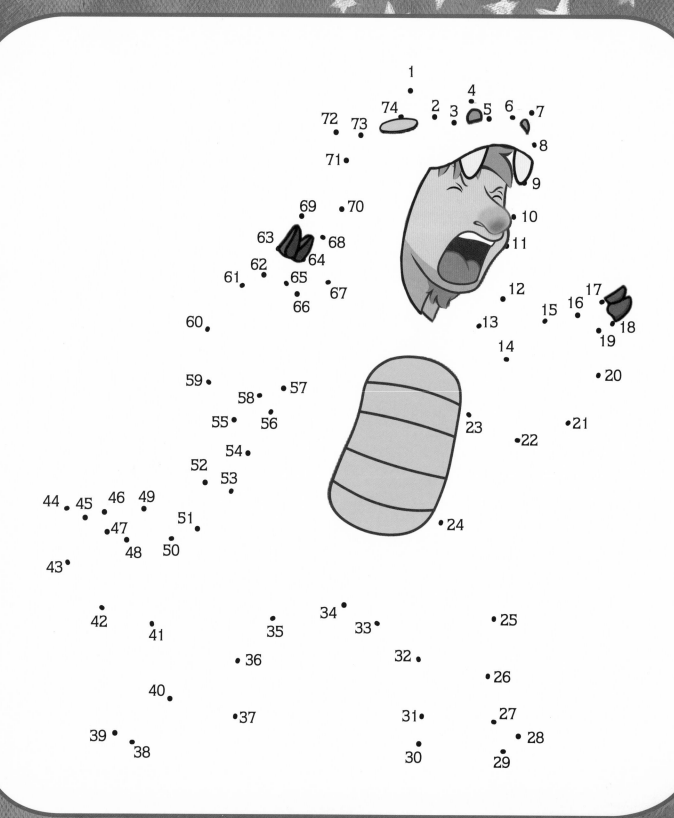

After that, Euclid and Llama have trouble falling asleep.

"Let's count sheep," Euclid says.

"Okay," Llama says. "One Euclid . . . two Euclids . . ."

And then Llama falls fast asleep.

Finish the scene by helping Llama count the sheep!

Answer:

The next morning, when Llama wakes up, he is hungry!

It is time for breakfast. Llama is excited to try more new foods.

Draw a yummy breakfast for Llama!

When Mama comes to pick up Llama, he is sad to go home.

He was having a lot of fun!

It was the best sleepover ever.

They will have to plan another sleepover soon!

Llama has to write a guest list. Circle the names of those attending his party!

E I G L G E
E U C L I D
M A M A L A
E L L M R R
L G I A O L
D M A D Y A

ANSWERS

Page 2

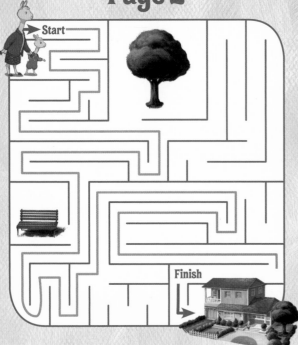

Page 6

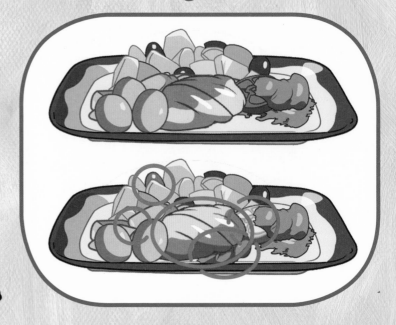

Page 7

18 fireflies

Page 13

17 sheep

Page 12

Page 15

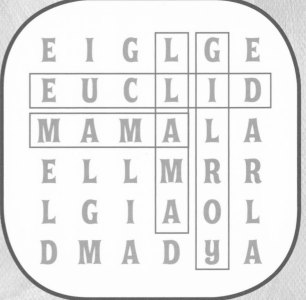

Pages 4-5

Page 9

Pages 10-11